The Lovables

in the Kingdom of Self-Esteem

Diana Loomans
Illustrated by Kim Howard

H J KRAMER
Starseed Press
Tiburon, California

To Julia,
my golden child and inspiration,
and
to Virginia Satir,
the mother of self-esteem.
D.L.

To my father,
who encouraged me
throughout his life.
K.H.

I AM LOVABLE.

Hi, *lovable friend*! I'm Mona Monkey.
I live in the Kingdom of Self-Esteem,
Along with my friends, we're the Lovable Team.
Come right along, bring your huggable you,
We'd all like to meet you and talk to you, too.

The gates of the kingdom are opening wide,
As you say these words three times with pride:

"I'm lovable! I'm lovable! I'm lovable!"

So come with me, and you will see,
All of the lovable ways to be.

I AM COURAGEOUS.

A *roaring welcome to the kingdom*. I'm Lawrence Lion.
In our great kingdom, it is clear
That love and friends are always near.
So if you're feeling any fear,
Remember this and leave it here.

I AM CAPABLE.

Hellooo-hooo. I'm Owen Owl.
All the Lovables have gifts to share,
Because they're capable and they care.
You and your friends are talented, too.
What is something you love to do?

I LOVE TO LEARN.

I'm *waving hello to you. I'm Elena Elephant.*
Learning something new each day
Brings me joy along my way.
I'll bet that someone bright as you
Will love to learn your whole life through.

I LOVE TO PLAY AND HAVE FUN.

Ha-ha hi friend! We're Bobbi and Billy Bear.
We wrestle and play in a gentle way.
We giggle and laugh all through the day.
Playing and laughing is good for you, too.
So play every day like the Lovables do.

I TAKE CARE OF MY BODY.

Howdy. I'm Bernie Buffalo.
I love my body and eat only the best.
I make sure I get plenty of rest.
Treat your body with love every day,
And you'll go galloping on your way.

I TAKE CARE OF THE WORLD AROUND ME.

Hel-lo, *buddy-o*! I'm Buddy Beaver.
I care for river, sky, and land,
For all of nature is so grand.
To our world you, too, can give
Loving care so the Earth may live.

I LOVE OTHERS AS THEY ARE.

Oceans of hellos! I'm Daniel Dolphin.
All of the Lovables near and far
Are oh so lovable just as they are.
Love is the greatest gift you can give
To yourself, and to others, as long as you live.

I AM GENTLE AND STRONG.

Ahoy mates! I'm Wong Whale.
I'm the biggest and strongest Lovable of all.
I am gentle to others, both large and small.
You, too, can be strong, instead of tough.
You, too, can be gentle, instead of rough.

I LIKE TO SHARE WITH OTHERS.

Peace to you. I'm Diana Dove.
I like to spread peace both far and wide.
Sharing brings happiness from deep inside.
When you open your heart to give and to share,
You show your friends how much you care.

I AM KIND.

A *gentle welcome.* I'm Dana Deer.
I'm kind to my friends, and kind to me, too,
Because I'm important and so are you.
Treat yourself with love each day,
And you'll treat others in a kinder way.

I AM FULL OF JOY!

Oh *boy, oh joy*. I'm *Hilda Hippo*.
Hippoty hoo ha, hippoty hey,
My, oh my, it's a hippo-full day!
Joy is a special note that you sing,
When you open your heart and let your song ring.

I AM SPECIAL AND UNIQUE.

Hi, *special friend*! I'm Oscar Ostrich.
With such skinny legs, some say I'm absurd!
Still I know I'm a really neat bird.
You are special by just being you.
Love yourself and others will, too.

I AM PROUD TO BE ME.

Stripes ahoy! I'm Zena Zebra.
I feel proud to be who I am.
All of my stripes are really quite grand.
You are important with your own part to play,
So show who you are in your own special way.

I AM BEAUTIFUL.

Fan-tastic to meet you. I'm Pierre Peacock.

My feathers are beautiful as can be.
I spread them wide for all to see.
There is a secret that you, too, must know:
True beauty comes from an inner glow.

I AM POSITIVE.

A *huggable hello.* I'm Pema Panda.
Cheerfulness is the gift that I bring.
I look for the bright side in everything.
The positive things that you think and you say
Create your tomorrow in a better way.

I LIKE TO DO MY BEST!

A *soaring hi.* I'm Edgar Eagle.
I stretch my wings to their widest span.
I love to do the best that I can.
You have an eagle inside of you, too,
To help you fly high and carry you through.

I AM POLITE.

Whooah, Hellooah! I'm Harvey Horse.
In the kingdom we say thank you, I'm sorry, and please.
We choose words with kindness and prefer not to tease.
Show respect for others and you'll be aware
Of the many ways there are to care.

I AM COOPERATIVE.

Hello to you. I'm Katie Kangaroo.
I like to carry my baby Kyle.
Hopping together, we travel in style.
Cooperation is so grand,
When you work with others hand in hand.

I TRUST MYSELF.

Greetings! *I'm Greta Goat.*
I trust myself because, you see,
My very own best friend is me.
You have a best friend inside you, too,
To show you what is right and true.

I RESPECT MYSELF.

Oh, hello! I'm Ryan Rhino.
Inside myself I'm strong and clear,
I listen and act on what I hear.
Take what you know; let it show.
Your respect for yourself will grow and grow.

I AM CALM AND RELAXED.

You've spotted me! I'm Gina Giraffe.
I stay calm since I've learned to be
Relaxed and moving in harmony.
Take a deep breath, and see how it goes,
Relaxing yourself from your head to your toes.

I AM PEACEFUL INSIDE.

HH-*ee-ll-ll-oo*. I'm *Tanya Turtle*.
I like to pull my head deep into my shell,
There I find a quiet place where everything is well.
By becoming very still you can find it, too—
A place of peace that's inside of you.

I AM THANKFUL.

Baa-baallo. I'm Laura Lamb.
I give thanks for our Lovable Team,
And for the Kingdom of Self-Esteem.
I'm so thankful that you are here,
Because you're a gift that's very dear.

Whether you are big or small,
You are the greatest gift of all.
Now that you're part of our Lovable Team,
We'll always hold you in high esteem.

Day or night, it's always true,
The kingdom lives inside of you.
When you say these words three times in a row:
"I'm lovable! I'm lovable! I'm lovable!"
Your lovable self will magically grow.

We're the Lovable Team and our hearts are a-beam.
We live in the Kingdom of Self-Esteem!

Text Copyright © 1991 by Diana Loomans
Illustrations Copyright © 1991 Kim Howard
All rights reserved. No part of this book may be reproduced or utilized
in any form or by any means, electronic or mechanical, including
photocopying, recording, or by any information storage and retrieval system,
without permission in writing from the publisher.
H J Kramer Inc.
P.O. Box 1082
Tiburon, CA 94920

Library of Congress Cataloging in Publication Data
Loomans, Diana.
    The Lovables in the Kingdom of Self-Esteem / Diana Loomans :
illustrated by Kim Howard
        p.   cm.
    Summary: Various animals in the Kingdom of Self-Esteem illustrate the different
qualities that contribute to being lovable and having self-esteem.
    ISBN 0-915811-25-1
    [1. Self-respect—Fiction.   2. Love—Fiction   3. Animals
—Fiction   4. Stories in rhyme.] I. Howard, Kim, ill.   II. Title
PZO.3.L8618Lo   1991
|E|—dc20   90-52633
                                                                      CIP
                                                                      AC

Editor: Linda Kramer
Editorial Assistant: Nancy Carleton
Composition: Classic Typography
Book Production: Schuetge & Carleton
Printed in Singapore
20   19   18   17   16